Grow Up and Be YOU!

Written by
Anuj Dalal

Illustrated by
Srushti Shekatkar

Grow up and be you,
Blossom, just be true,

In a world with storms,
Let kindness brew.

Amidst a world divided, seek harmony,

Because you are born in a time
of moonlit fantasy.

Aim high, aim far, beyond the sky,

The world's waiting for you to fly.

For those who express,
their light unfolds,

In their truths,
the world beholds.

Change the world,
Let your light shine through,

Grow up and be uniquely you.

Grow up,
speak soft but not still,

Embrace yourself,
let your heart fill.

Count your blessings,
Be thankful each day,

In every high and low,
find a silver ray.

As you journey,
true and free,

Remember fun, a must,
you see.

With smiles wide,
let happiness run,

Life is a treasure,
for everyone.

In this world,
you will learn and grow,

But also share what the previous
generation does not yet know!

As I write this tale so true,

Remember,
your legacy is up to you!